Bear Hug

by Laurence Pringle

Illustrated by
Kate Salley Palmer

Published by Boyds Mills Press
A Highlights Company
815 Church Street
Honesdale, Pennsylvania 18431
Printed in China
Visit our Web site at www.boydsmillspress.com

Publisher Cataloging-in-Publication Data (U.S.)

Pringle, Laurence.
    Bear hug / by Laurence Pringle ; illustrations by
Kate Salley Palmer. — 1st ed.
[32] p. : col. ill. ; cm.
Summary: When Mom needs a day to herself, Dad takes the children on a
camping trip.
ISBN 1-56397-876-8
1. Camping—Fiction. 2. Father and child—Fiction. I. Palmer, Kate Salley. II. Title
 [E] 21   AC   2003
2002105793

First edition, 2003
The text of this book is set in 14-point Clearface.

10 9 8 7 6 5 4 3 2 1

For Samantha and Gillian Jacobi, the granddaughters whom a friend,
Peter Jacobi, loves to hug

—L. P.

For all our family dogs—Vee, Kayla, Maggie, Newberry, and especially the
late Pepper, for taking me along on their adventures in the woods and at the lake

—K. S. P.

"Good-bye, Jesse. Good-bye, Becky." Mom hugged us really tight. She needed a day to herself to finish writing a book, so Dad was taking us camping.

We waved to Mom as we set out down the street in the early morning light.

Becky and I had never camped before. We were excited—and a little scared.

"Are there bears at Black Bear Lake?" I asked.

"No," said Dad. "The lake got that name a long time ago."

The car engine purred. The tires hummed. And Dad began to sing: "Over the river and through the woods, a-camping we will go. The car knows the way and won't lead us astray, so to Black Bear Lake we go!"

Maybe the car did know the way. It drove and drove for many miles until it stopped by a path that led into the woods. A sign read, "Black Bear Lake—One Mile."

"Okay," said Dad. "Everybody helps." We all put on our backpacks. Becky and I each carried a sleeping bag and some food. Becky brought along her favorite stuffed animal. Dad carried much, much more.

The trail led us up, up, up into the wild woods. Then
it led us down, down, down, toward something that shined
like silver through the trees ahead.
   "Welcome to Black Bear Lake," Dad said with a big smile.

Soon we reached the lakeshore and looked out over the water. There were no houses. Black Bear Lake was surrounded by wild forest.

We hiked along the shore until we reached a camping place among the trees. A circle of stones marked the spot to build a fire.

Dad showed us how to find dead twigs and branches for our campfire. Becky and I made a woodpile while Dad pitched the tent.

It was only midafternoon, but we unrolled our sleeping bags in the tent. This way our home for the night was ready whenever we wanted to go to bed.

"Now," said Dad, "it's time to meet our neighbors."

Becky and I looked around. "I don't see anyone," I said.

Dad said, "Me, neither. But I hear someone in the woods. Let's see who it is."

We walked toward the chattering sound. A red squirrel seemed to be talking to us from a pine tree. When we reached the tree, the squirrel twitched its tail rapidly and scampered to a higher branch.

"It's okay, squirrel," I said, "we won't hurt you."

The squirrel kept chattering at us.

Next we took a walk along the lakeshore. Dragonflies hovered over the water and darted after mosquitoes. Birds with forked tails swooped by.

"Those are barn swallows," said Dad, "and those birds twittering high in the sky are chimney swifts."

A frog was so tame that it sat in Becky's hand for a moment without leaping away.

"Maybe," Dad said, "that frog has never seen people before."

Farther along the shore we found trees that had been cut down by a beaver's sharp teeth. I kept a beaver-chewed twig to show Mom.

By the time we hiked back to camp, the sun was low in the sky, hidden by trees. Dad made a little pile of dry leaves and small twigs, then let me strike a match to start our campfire. We stuck hot dogs on the ends of long sticks and cooked them over the hot fire. They were the same kind of hot dogs we eat at home, but they tasted so much better here in the woods by Black Bear Lake.

For dessert we ate toasted marshmallows. Becky cooked hers until they were plump and brown. I let mine catch fire, then blew out the flames. This made the marshmallows gooey on the inside, crispy black on the outside.

By then it was almost dark—time, Dad said, to meet
more neighbors. We left the glow of the fire and made
our way down to the edge of the water. In the day the
lake had sparkled with sunbeams. Now it winked with the
reflections of countless stars in the sky.

We sat close together on a log, facing the water. We
watched and waited.

The birds had gone to sleep. Now bats swooped by,
hunting for insects over the water.

"Shush," said Dad, "just listen." We listened and listened.

Becky whispered, "I don't hear anything."

"Yeah," said Dad. "No cars, no voices, no radio or TV. Just quiet."

We kept listening. We had never heard such silence. But then it was broken—by a sound that sent a shiver up my spine. A deep ghostly call came from the forest on the other side of the lake.

"*Hoohoo-hoohoo . . . hoohoo-hoohooaw.*"

It came again. "*Hoohoo-hoohoo . . . hoohoo-hoohooaw.*"

"Is it a bear?" Becky whispered.

"No," said Dad. "Hush for a minute."

Suddenly the call from across the lake was answered by one that came from the woods right behind us. *"HOOHOO-HOOHOO . . . HOOHOO-HOOHOOAW."*

We all turned to look but saw only the glow of our campfire.

"We have another neighbor," Dad said softly. "A barred owl. It's talking to another barred owl across the lake."

Dad took a deep breath, cupped his hands around his mouth, and called out, "HOOHOO-HOOHOO . . . HOOHOOAW!"

We stayed still, listening. For a moment all we could hear was our breathing. Then there was a rush of air, a rustle of feathers. With slow wing beats, the owl flew right over our heads and vanished into the darkness.

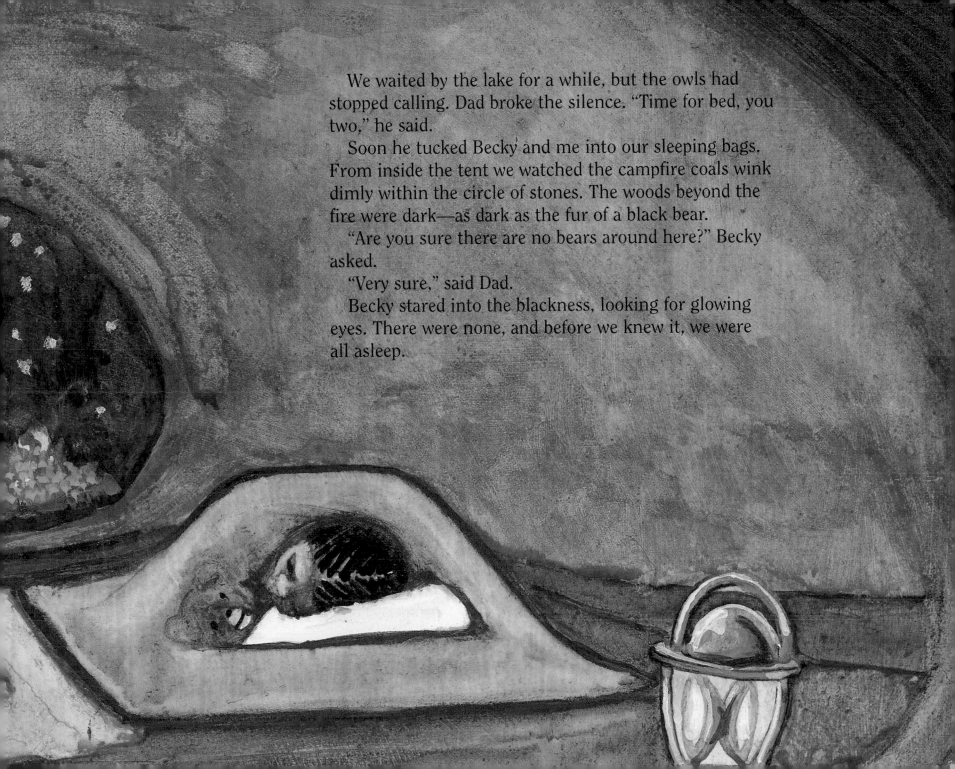

We waited by the lake for a while, but the owls had stopped calling. Dad broke the silence. "Time for bed, you two," he said.

Soon he tucked Becky and me into our sleeping bags. From inside the tent we watched the campfire coals wink dimly within the circle of stones. The woods beyond the fire were dark—as dark as the fur of a black bear.

"Are you sure there are no bears around here?" Becky asked.

"Very sure," said Dad.

Becky stared into the blackness, looking for glowing eyes. There were none, and before we knew it, we were all asleep.

When we woke the next morning, the lake was hidden by fog. Water drops were strung like jewels on spiderwebs along the shore.

We warmed ourselves by the fire, and with oatmeal that Dad cooked. Then he took down the tent while Becky and I poured water on the fire to put it out. "Let's be good neighbors," said Dad, and we left the campsite neat and clean.

We said good-bye to the red squirrel and the frogs. As we got ready to hike up the trail, Becky said, "I want to come back and bring Mom."

Feeling brave after our night in the woods, I said, "Now I wish we *had* seen a bear."

"Well," said Dad, "there is *one* bear." He roared and gave us both a great big bear hug.